HOWL

Big, toothy thanks for the ferociousness of Maggie, Kate, Miri and Iris. You have howls as big as your hearts. —Kat

For Zoe and Bridget, and everyone who has had or is having one of those days. —EB

The illustrations in this book are made with coloured pencil, chalk pastel, wax crayon, as well as digital drawing and retouching.
Typeset in Adobe Caslon

Scribble, an imprint of Scribe Publications
18–20 Edward Street, Brunswick, Victoria 3056, Australia
2 John Street, Clerkenwell, London, WC1N 2ES, United Kingdom
3754 Pleasant Ave, Suite 100, Minneapolis, Minnesota 55409 USA

Text © Kat Patrick 2020
Illustrations © Evie Barrow 2020

First published by Scribble 2020

This book is printed on FSC™ certified paper from responsibly managed forests, ensuring that the supply chain from forest to end-user is chain of custody certified. Printed and bound in China by Imago.

9781925849806 (ANZ hardback)
9781912854905 (UK hardback)
9781950354450 (North American hardback)

Catalogue records for this title are available from the National Library of Australia and the British Library.

scribblekidsbooks.com
scribblekidsbooks

MIX
Paper from responsible sources
FSC
www.fsc.org   FSC™ C005748

HOWL

written by

KAT PATRICK

illustrated by

EVIE BARROW

SCRIBBLE

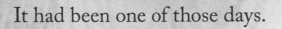

It had been one of those days.

First of all,
the sun was the wrong shape,
in a sky that was too blue.

Then, Maggie's shoes would not go on properly.
Her socks were even worse.

The silly pencil wasn't working –
all the squiggles were too squiggly,
or not squiggly enough.

Finally,
the spaghetti was too long,

and the pajamas were the wrong kind
of pajama.

The moon was so bright through the windows
no one wanted to sleep.

Maggie almost exploded.
So did Mom.

To top it all,
Maggie's two front teeth decided
it was the right time to fall out.

But, after lights out,
two small fangs grew back in their place.
She could touch their sharpness with her tongue.

Maggie began to have wolfish thoughts.

She sprouted itchy little hairs,
her ears felt extra pointy,
and her hands curled into paws.

Maggie snuck out of bed
to dance under the luxurious moon.

Her shadow looked perfectly ferocious
and in the light each hair turned bright silver.

More than anything,
Maggie wanted to howl.

She tipped her head back,
turned her ears towards the moon…

but nothing came out.
Not even the smallest snarl.

Meanwhile,
through the kitchen window,
a cold bit of moonlight spilled onto Mom's toe.

Slowly it covered her whole foot.
Mom felt a little strange…

…then stranger still.
Her nose twitched and her teeth sharpened.

Something tickled her throat.
Mom began to have wolfish thoughts.

'If I am a Mom,'
she howled.
'Then I am also a wolf.'

OOOWWWLLL

Maggie couldn't believe her ears.
Wolf Mom's big teeth shone in the moonlight.

'How did you do that?'
Maggie asked.

Wolf Mom showed her.
'Take a deep breath.
Count to seven,
which is ten in human breaths,
and imagine your biggest feelings
flying into the sky.'

'If I am a girl,'
Maggie howled.
'Then I am also a wolf.'

OOWWWWWLLLL

OOWWWL

OoOOOOo

Together they howled so loudly
it woke up Maggie's friend Iris,
who lived eleven houses away.

Wolf Mom grinned.

'Wolves can do other things, too.'

They prowled around the
garden at least four times,
then once more for luck –
extra fast.

They used their big ears
to listen carefully to the darkness,
where things were awake or dreaming very loudly.

They used their powerful noses
to sniff the magic on the evening breeze,
feeling the fur bristle on their long tails.

They used their enormous breath
to huff and puff shapes into the clouds,
flashing their eyes like the stars.

Best of all,
they danced wildly under the moon.

It felt good to be a wolf.

As the moon ducked behind the trees,
Wolf Girl yawned.

She scratched her snout
and decided it must be time for bed.

It felt good to be Maggie, too.

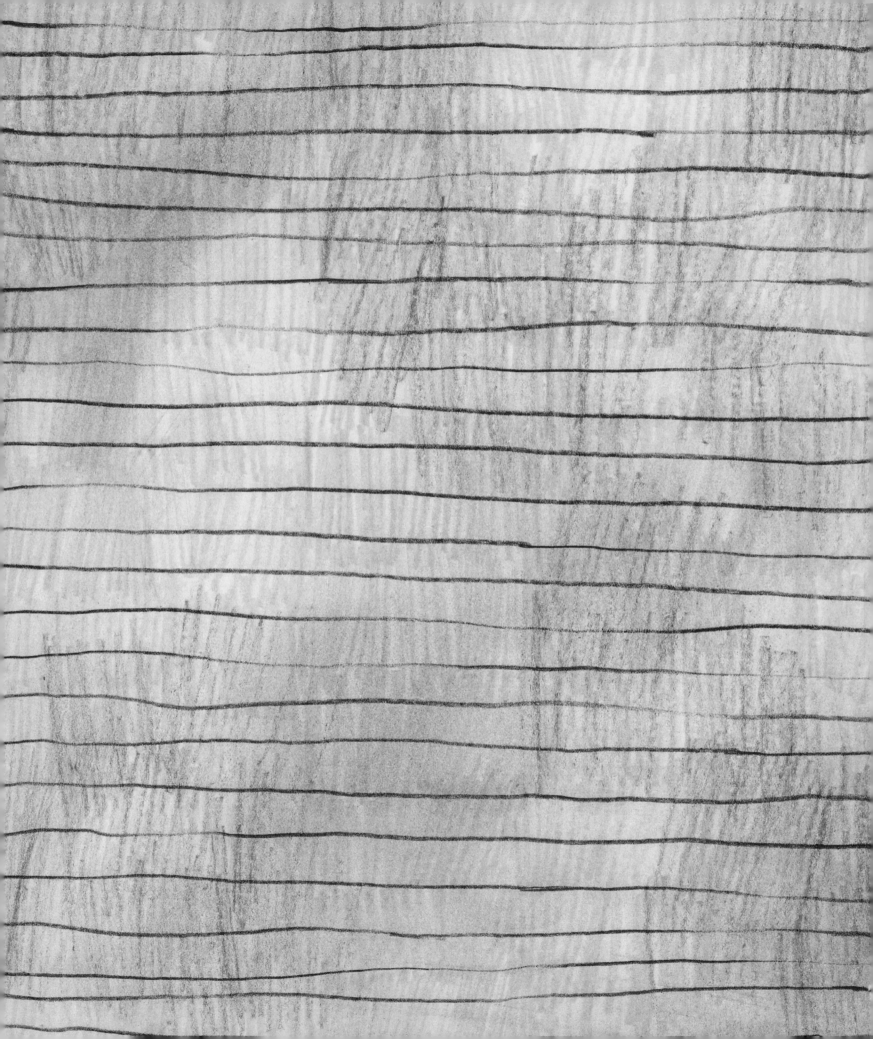